Dec,2014

ALGONQUIN AREA PUBLIC LIBRARY DISTRICT

W9-BMQ-212

WITHDRAWN

Algonquin Area Public Library
Eastgate Branch
115 Eastgate Dr
Algonquin, IL 60102
www.aapld.org

Hissy Fitz

Hissy Fitz

By
Patrick Jennings

ILLUSTRATED BY
Michael Allen Austin

EGMONT
Publishing
NEW YORK

EGMONT

We bring stories to life

First published by Egmont Publishing, 2015
443 Park Avenue South, Suite 806
New York, NY 10016

Text copyright © 2015 by Patrick Jennings
Illustrations copyright © 2015 by Michael Allen Austin
All rights reserved

1 3 5 7 9 8 6 4 2

www.egmontusa.com
www.patrickjennings.com
www.MichaelAllenAustin.com

Library of Congress Cataloging-in-Publication Data
Jennings, Patrick
Hissy Fitz / by Patrick Jennings ; illustrated by Michael Allen Austin.
pages cm
Summary: Hissy, a sleep-deprived British shorthair cat in the extremely noisy
Fitz household, recounts his frustrating day trying to find a place to sleep where
people--particularly an annoying three-year-old human--will not bother him.
ISBN 978-1-60684-596-7 (hardcover)
1. British shorthair--Juvenile fiction. 2. Cats--Juvenile fiction. 3. Families--Juvenile
fiction. 4. Sleep deprivation--Juvenile fiction. [1. Cats--Fiction. 2. Family life--Fiction.
3. Sleep--Fiction.] I. Austin, Michael Allen, illustrator. II. Title.

PZ7.J4298715Hi 2015
813.6--dc23
[Fic]

2014034627

eBook ISBN 978-1-60684-597-4

Printed in the United States of America

All rights reserved. No part of this publication may be reproduced, stored
in a retrieval system, or transmitted, in any form or by any means,
electronic, mechanical, photocopying, or otherwise, without the prior
written permission of the publisher and the copyright holder.

FOR LOUISE

Contents

1.

Clueless Georgie

"Hissy! I'm home!" Georgie yells as she bursts through the front door.

I like Georgie. I do. I've known her since she was born, more than eight years ago, when I was just a kitten. I was there when she smiled for the first time, when she first sat up by herself, when she said her first word (*meow*), and when she took her first step. We were about the same size then. She has grown much larger since, larger than me, and much, much noisier. But I am still older. I will always be older.

My question is, After all we've been through together, why does she still treat me like a kitten?

Why, when we've known each other so long, does she insist on waking me from my all-important sleep?

A moment ago, I was happily napping on the windowsill in the sunshine, dreaming I was flying through the air, catching sparrows in my claws. Now I'm awake. Georgie woke me.

I wouldn't do that to her.

I open one eye.

She presses her face into my soft, silver-blue fur. "Oh, how I missed you, little Hissy!" she squeals too near my ear.

I open my other eye, and growl: *Grrrrrrrrrr!*

"And you missed me, too! Awww!"

Georgie can't always tell the difference between a growl and a purr.

I bare my claws, sink them into the windowsill, and begin to wriggle free. She senses that I'm trying to get away and squeezes tighter. I raise my hackles and let out a long hiss.

Hssssssssss!

It does the trick. Georgie lets go of me and plops down on the bench beneath the window.

"You know what happened at school today?" she asks.

I do not.

"Ethan was making towers with his base ten blocks."

She looked shocked. I have no idea what base ten blocks are, but she gives me little scratches between my ears as she talks — which I quite enjoy — so I purr my encouragement: *Prrrrrrrrrr!*

It's simple. I hiss when she does something I don't like; I purr when she does something I like. Why doesn't she learn?

"Of course, I told him he shouldn't, but he said he should, so I said, 'I mean, you're not *supposed* to,' but he did it anyway!"

I tip my head upward, trying to guide her hand to my cheeks. I love having my cheeks stroked, a fact I've tried to impress upon her for years. She slides her hand down my neck, then glides it over my back toward my tail. This is not what I want. I do not like her near my tail. She has a habit of weaving it through her fingers, which tugs.

"Ms. Seven saw him and asked him to take the towers apart. They're for doing math, not for building towers, you know."

I did not.

She slumps backward onto the bench's plump throw pillows. I slip my tail from her grasp, jump down from the sill, and rub my cheeks against her arm. Sometimes I have to do everything myself.

She gives a big yawn, stretching her arms out to her side. Her eyelids lower. She often takes a nap after school. In my opinion, human beings do not nap enough, especially the little ones. All that racing around, hopping, and squawking would certainly wear me out. Children should take more naps than cats do.

I curl up beside her. She smiles sleepily. She likes when I nap with her. So do I. As I said, I like Georgie. I also like napping, and I almost never get enough sleep. It's because I live in this house, with the noisy Fitz family, with this noisy, clueless girl.

Georgie's breathing slows and deepens. Just like that, she's out. I'm almost there, too, until . . .

"Hissy cat!" Zeb yells as he races through the door, his fists pumping, his chin forward. Zeb is one of Georgie's three-year-old brothers. The untamed one. As usual, he's looking for trouble.

I'm not, though I can bring it when necessary.

It's necessary.

2.

Human Twins

Hssssssss! I say.

I spring from Georgie's side and cross the room in three quick bounds. My destination is the big square bed in the master bedroom. Zeb can't get at me when I'm under it.

"I wouldn't chase the cat, Zeb," says Georgie's dad. He comes in behind his son, holding the hand of his other one. "Hissy doesn't like it."

He's right, Hissy doesn't, but Zeb doesn't listen to his dad.

I hiss again as I exit the room—*Hssssssssss!*—then fly up the stairs. Down the hall, I duck into the master bedroom, where I dive under the big square bed.

Zeb clambers up the stairs. "Cat!" he cries. "Hissy cat! Where ar-r-r-re you?"

He toddles into the room. He knows my hiding places.

Hssssssssss! I say again. He really can't take a hint. He's worse than Georgie.

He peeks under the bed. "There you are, Hissy cat. Come here. Come on."

Is he kidding?

When I don't come out, he climbs onto the bed and starts hopping up and down. He hiccups my name each time he lands.

I lay my snout on my paws. It's no wonder I have trouble sleeping in this house.

Light footsteps skip up the stairs, then Abe steps into the doorway. The other twin. He's wearing his stuffed-rabbit puppet, Medium Sad Guy, on his hand. Its long silver ears dangle almost to the floor. Abe's head tilts up and down in time with his brother's bouncing.

Abe is a nice, quiet boy, who never wakes me or chases me or jumps up and down on my head. Are all human twins so opposite?

"HISS-sy! HISS-sy! HISS-sy!" Zeb chants.

Heavier footsteps on the stairs. Dad's.

"Come here, Zeb," he says, entering the room. He steps past Abe. "Give the cat a break."

I appreciate this, though Dad, who's a carpenter, didn't exactly give the cat a break today. He made a terrible racket out in his backyard workshop with his hammers and his shrieking, grinding power tools. And his radio. His rock 'n' roll.

Again, Zeb doesn't listen to his dad. He continues to hop and chant.

Dad steps up to the bed. "Come on," he says. "Jump to Daddy."

Zeb hits the bed one more time. Dad grunts. I assume he caught the boy, so I shoot for the door. I swerve past Abe's ankles into the hall, then down the stairs.

Georgie appears when I reach the bottom. I guess she couldn't sleep, either.

"What's the matter, Hissy?" she asks. "Is Zeb bothering you?"

Yes, Zeb is bothering me.

She bends down and picks me up. I don't mind being picked up. I don't love it, but if done properly, it's not horrible. Georgie doesn't do it properly. She turns me onto my back, with my belly up, which is how humans carry their babies. It is not how cats carry theirs. It makes me nervous. And annoyed. I growl. *Grrrrrrrrr!*

She scratches my chest with her finger.

I wriggle.

She holds me tighter.

I hiss.

Hsssssssss!

"Oh, Hissy," she says,
"why are you in a bad mood?"

I'm not in a bad mood. I'm in
a mad mood. I bare my claws and twist.

"Ow!" she says, loosening her grip.

I fall perfectly to the floor, onto all four paws. I
spring away. I am using all the energy I've saved up.

"You little rascal!" Georgie calls after me. "You
scratched me! Come back here and say you're
sorry!"

I won't be doing that.

3.

Dad Drops the Ball

I slink into the kitchen, my ears twisting, listening
for Zeb. He's up in his room, pounding on something. The boy takes after his father. *Bam, bam,
bam!* I don't understand this drive to hammer.
Maybe if I had thumbs . . .

I make for my food and water dishes. One is
nearly empty; the other needs freshening. Dad's
been so busy in his workshop that he forgot about
the cat's needs. He didn't forget about his own,
however. He dipped into the kitchen several times

to snack and refill his water bottle from the spout in the refrigerator door. I doubt Dad would care to drink water that had been sitting in a bowl all day.

I pick up a few kibbles with my tongue then crunch them. They taste as they always do: dry and slightly fishy. I'd prefer actual fish, but I don't have enough energy to go out and find and kill one.

I still need water, so I pad into the bathroom. The toilet seat is down. Rats. I won't risk checking the upstairs toilets. Not with Zeb on the loose.

It drizzled a little this morning, so I can probably find a pool of rainwater outside. I duck through my door and run down the back porch steps into the yard. The grass is slightly damp. I lick the moisture off a few blades. It's a start. I roll around in the grass then lie down and lick my fur. This is grooming and drinking at the same time.

My eyelids feel heavy. Maybe I could steal a little nap here in the grass before—

"There you are!" Georgie says, pushing open the kitchen door.

If she comes near me, I will smack her. I know that's not nice, but it's how I feel.

"I filled your food dish," she says. She sets it down on the porch.

Okay, now I feel bad.

I scurry over to it. Oh, she opened a *can*! It's Salmon Supper and tastes more like fish than the dry stuff does. She scratches my head as I lap it up. This is more like it. This is good. I love Georgie.

Bang! This is Zeb slamming the door behind him as he emerges from the kitchen.

"Hissy cat!" he roars. His hands are curled up like claws. He hisses. Which is my thing.

Hsssssssss! I say.

I abandon the food with a heavy heart, but in a hurry. Zeb is a monster.

I consider dashing away across the lawn, scaling the fence, and disappearing into the neighborhood. But the neighborhood is dangerous during the day. Automobiles, dogs, and kids everywhere. I'd never find a place to sleep, either. Too noisy. Wherever you find humans, you will find noise.

Instead, I shoot through Zeb's legs and back through my door into the kitchen. Georgie neglected to close the pantry door after she got the can of food, so I slip inside. I leap over a row of large cans on the floor and hunker down. I feel my pulse in my throat.

The door bangs again and Zeb's heavy feet bang on the linoleum. *Bang, bang, bang!*

"Leave Hissy alone, Zeb!" Georgie says. The door opens again and she steps inside. "I just got him calmed down. He was real mad after you chased him upstairs. He even scratched me."

Zeb roars again. He's a wild animal. He shouldn't be allowed inside. He should be an outside boy.

He runs from the room. I've escaped him. For now.

"Hissy?" Georgie whispers, peeking into the pantry.

She knows my hiding places, too.

I'd be mad if she weren't holding the food dish. I mew.

She giggles. "I thought you might be in here."

She pulls the door almost shut behind her, then crouches. I leap back over the cans and dive into the Salmon Supper.

Georgie scratches my back. I prefer the head, but I let it pass. I do complain when she weaves my tail in her fingers.

Hssssssss!

"Shhh," she says. "We don't want Zeb to find out where we are."

She's right. She brought me food. She's protecting me from the toddler. She can tug my tail all she wants. She's only human, after all.

4.

Howls of the Monster

I'm now fed and lying on Georgie's lap. She's on her bed. I'd love to sleep; however, Georgie will not stop yakking.

"In the library today Mr. Fairchild read a story about a cat named Due Date that lived in a library. It was called *Library Kitty*, which isn't a very creative title, is it? The cat lived in the library, and was really sweet, and everyone loved her, and then one day she disappeared, and everyone got so sad, even the people who didn't really like cats. There are

people like that, you know, Hissy. Not everybody
loves cats the way me and Tillie do."

Tillie is Georgie's best friend. She has a white cat
named Igloo, whom I sometimes prowl with during
the night.

As Georgie relates the story of the missing
library cat, she strokes me. She seldom pays
attention to what she's doing while she's yakking,
so I guide her hand toward my cheeks. I purr loudly
to show my approval. *Prrrrrrrrrr!*

"At the end, Due Date just walks into the library followed by the cutest little baby kitties you ever saw! Me and Tillie thought that was a perfect ending, though we both had a feeling the story was heading that way. Ethan made a sound with his mouth—what do you call that when you make your lips go . . ." She blows through her closed lips, which makes a spluttery sound.

I don't know what you call that. Unattractive?

"He didn't like the ending. He didn't like the *story*, because he doesn't like cats. Like I said, not everyone does. Mr. Fairchild asked him to go sit at a table by himself, and I guess he found a piece of a broken eraser on it and put it in his mouth and started choking. It was pretty funny, but then scary, because his face turned all red. Mr. Fairchild rushed over and gave him the Heimlich, and Ethan went *hunh!* The eraser shot out of his mouth and landed on the table. That was pretty funny, too. And scary. But we all laughed."

Maybe it's the steady stream of Georgie's talking, or maybe it's the expert petting I'm forcing her to do, but I feel drowsy. I yawn a huge, fang-baring, tongue-curling yawn and stretch out my toes. My eyelids slide shut.

"*Yowwooooooooooo! Daaaa-deeee!*" howls Zeb from somewhere. "*Yowwooooooooooo!*"

I'm wide awake.

"That's Zebby," Georgie says, brushing me off her lap and jumping to the floor. "It sounds like he's really hurt." She pulls her heavy backpack away from the door—she put it there to keep him out—then runs out of the room.

I move to the warm spot she left behind. Maybe I can get back to where I was before Zeb started screaming.

Yes, he's still screaming.

Heh, heh.

I know it's not polite to be happy about it. Maybe it's just a mild injury that will prevent him from chasing cats for a while.

Heh.

5.

Peanut Butter

I nod off, and, just like that, I'm in flight again. I swoop down from the branch of a tall tree, a fat robin in my sights. I bare my claws and—

Woof! Woof! Woof-woof-woof! Woof!

I wake up on the bed. The dog wasn't in my dream. I rise up to the window and peek outside. Ethan and his huge puppy, Peanut Butter, are coming up the sidewalk. They live down the street. Ethan needs to train the beast not to bark. He doesn't even try to shush him.

I leap up and screech, *Yeeeowwwwooorrrr!*

Peanut Butter gallops into our yard. He's loose, of course. Ethan never leashes him.

"Can you keep that dog quiet?" a voice from below me asks. It's Georgie, on the front porch. "Zeb had an accident."

And your cat is trying to sleep.

"Really?" Ethan asks. "What happened to him?"

"That's none of your business. Can you make Peanut Butter be quiet?"

"Not really. He doesn't listen to me. What happened to Zeb?"

"I'm not listening to you, either— *Help!*"

Peanut Butter has bounded up the steps and is licking Georgie's face with his long, pink tongue.

Peanut Butter is a golden retriever. Though he's only a year old, he probably weighs as much as Georgie. His tongue alone is enough to knock her over.

I hiss at him to stop. *Hsssssssss!*

He stops licking, looks up, and starts barking.

I hiss again, with extra nastiness. *HSSSSSSSSSS!*

He barks louder and starts bucking—front feet, hind feet, front feet, hind feet. He looks ridiculous. Undignified. Now that he's leaving Georgie alone, I settle back down to watch the show.

Zeb comes tearing around from the back of the house, yelling, "Peanut Butter!" He makes a beeline toward the hound. I notice he has a knot on his forehead.

Woof? Peanut Butter answers, understandably frightened. He's met Zeb. Zeb loves pulling Peanut Butter's long, golden hair. He loves tugging his lovable, floppy ears, and his curved, furry tail.

Peanut Butter turns and flees.

Zeb flies after him, screaming, "Come, dog! Come! Come, dog!"

Ethan chases after him, yelling, "Don't chase Peanut Butter, Zeb! Stop chasing him!"

Georgie runs after Ethan, hollering, "Leave my brother alone, Ethan! Leave him alone!"

Just another quiet afternoon in the neighborhood.

I step down onto Georgie's bed, then up onto her dresser. It's painted pink and has a mirror attached. I look at myself. I look tired. Frazzled. I look like I feel. I need rest. Georgie and Zeb are gone. Maybe I can steal a quick nap. I curl up right there on Georgie's dresser, in a pool of afternoon sun. I take a deep, shuddery breath, close my itchy eyes, and exhale slowly.

The lawn mower across the street roars to life.

Dogs howl at it from somewhere.

A crow and a gull scream at each other.

Downstairs, Dad starts the washing machine.

I won't be stealing anything.

6.

Smart Kid

I go down to the kitchen in the hope that Georgie
freshened my water dish. Dad is there with Abe.
They're sitting at the table, having a snack:
crackers, peanut butter, apple slices. I don't
understand human tastes.

Abe eats with one hand. His other is in his
rabbit puppet. He eyes me as I creep along the
cabinets toward my dishes. Dish, actually. My food
dish is probably still in the pantry. I left a little
Salmon Supper in it for later. The stagnant water
in my water dish has been freshened. As I drink, I
listen in.

"How many time-outs did your brother get today?" Dad asks.

"Six," Abe says.

Dad sighs. "How many did you get?"

He's joking. He knows Abe never gets time-outs.

"Zero," Abe says.

"Did you build anything?"

"A castle."

"How many turrets?"

"Four."

"Did Zeb leave it alone?"

"Nope."

"Was that one of his time-outs?"

"Yep."

"Did you nap?"

"A little."

"Zeb wake you up?"

"Yep."

I feel his pain.

"Want to do some hammering in the workshop?" Dad asks.

"Yep."

Add hammering to the barking dogs, shrieking birds, grating lawn mower . . . I may as well give up.

Can one give up on sleep?

Heavy steps on the back stairs. Zeb has returned. I dash into the pantry. He opens the back door, then slams it behind him. He clomps across the kitchen.

"One cracker at a time, Zeb," I hear Dad say. "Don't stuff them in your mouth. You'll choke."

I hear a cough.

"Oh, Zeb!" Dad says. "Cracker crumbs everywhere!"

"Time-out?" Abe asks.

"Zeb, sit down," Dad says. "Don't put your feet on the chair. Sit on your bottom. On your *bottom.*"

A chair crashes to the floor.

"Now a time-out?" Abe asks.

"We're at home, Abe," Dad says. "Mom doesn't want us to do time-outs at home. We're supposed to clean up our messes. Come on, Zeb. Help me pick up the chair, then we'll wipe up those crumbs."

"I want to hammer!" Zeb shouts.

It's something Dad does with the kids after school. Dad wears noise-canceling earmuffs. How do I get a pair of those?

"After you clean up," Dad says.

Georgie comes through the door, puffing. "There you are! Daddy, he was chasing Peanut Butter again! He chased him all the way down the street!"

Dad sighs.

The washing machine shuts off.

"The clothes need to go in the dryer," Abe says.

"Let's go do some hammering!" Dad says.

"Yay!" Zeb cheers.

"You didn't clean up," Abe says.

"Don't push your brother, Zeb," Dad says. "Let's all clean up so we can go hammer, okay?"

"But you're doing all the cleaning up, Daddy," Georgie says.

"Let's all help each other," he replies. "Zeb? Can you help?"

Zeb runs to the door, opens it, slams it. From the backyard he yells, "Tool Time! Tool Time!"

There's a silence. I lick my Salmon Supper.

"Zeb?" Dad calls, walking across the room in his heavy work boots. "Zeb? No Tool Time till we clean up, Zeb. Zeb?"

He goes out the door.

The pantry door opens. I squint at the light.

It's Abe. He steps inside and peers over the cans at me. He knows my hiding places, too. Everyone knows my hiding places. There are only so many places to hide in this house.

He sits down on the floor, cross-legged, with Medium Sad Guy in his lap. I step over the cans. Abe understands things his older sister hasn't learned. Don't go after a cat. Let the cat come to you.

I go to him. I curl up in his lap, on top of Medium Sad Guy.

Abe holds his hand up over me. He also knows that you don't pet a cat. You let the cat pet you.

I raise my head up into his hand and guide it where I want it to go. Which is to my cheeks. He massages them with his fingers.

I hear hammering coming from the shed, and Dad yelling, "No Tool Time until we clean up, Zeb! We need to clean up first!"

"Tool Time!" Zeb hollers between bangs. "Tool Time!"

I look up at Abe. He lifts an eyebrow. His eyes look tired. We could both use a nap.

Bang! Bang! Bang! goes Zeb's hammer.

"We're in a time-out," Abe says.

Smart kid.

7.

The Noisiest Creature

Three hammers hammer in my head. Or so it feels.

Bang! Bang! Bang!—over and over and over and over and over . . .

I can't take it. I *will* not take it!

Forget about the dangers. I'm leaving the pantry, leaving Abe's strokes, leaving the property.

I go out my door and slink through the grass to the fir tree beside the house. Through the open door of the workshop, I see Dad, Georgie, and Zeb swinging hammers. The kids have small hammers and are not driving nails; they're just banging their hammers on blocks of wood. Dad is wearing his earmuffs . . . and smiling. Hammering cheers him up.

Not me.

I shimmy up the fir tree, along the sturdy branch to the neighboring house's oak tree.

A young married couple, Kim and Gil, live next door. Gil often works on cars in his driveway. More noise. He's below me, his head under the hood of a car. The engine is running. He walks around and sits in the driver's seat and guns the motor. *Grrr-RRRRRRRRR!*

I run along the branch to another tree, then to another, till the noise of Gil's car fades. Of course, there's plenty of noise from other cars in the neighborhood. And trucks. And buses. In fact, a school bus is rattling down our street at this very moment. It comes to a stop, then, *Beep! Beep! Beep! Beep!* Some kids step off the bus, then run down the street yelling.

Humans are the noisiest creatures alive.

I'm not sure there is any escape. At least, not until late at night.

I can't wait that long. Besides, I can't always get to sleep at night. It's a cat's time to hunt. Even house cats—who don't need to hunt—feel this nocturnal urge. It's an instinct.

None of my friends have as much trouble sleeping, but then none of them live with Zeb. Or with Dad's tools. Or with Georgie. They leave me too tired to sleep. Too wound up. The more I try, the harder it becomes.

Georgie's grandma has this problem. She doesn't sleep well, either. She calls it insomnia. I guess I have insomnia, too.

I stay off the ground as I make my way through the neighborhood. I walk along on fences, branches, cars. I climb trees, leap onto rooftops. I hesitate when I come upon a bird on a perch. I crouch. I stalk. I pounce. I don't catch it. That's all right. I'm fed. If I keep up all this exercise, however, I will soon need to eat again.

Before long I am at Igloo's house. I see him lying on his family's couch, in the sunshine. He's sprawled out on his back, his paws resting on his

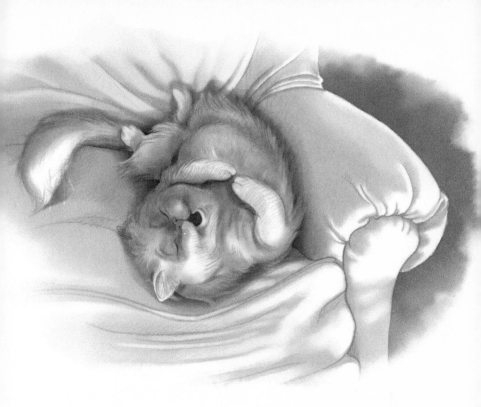

chest. That's a deep-sleep pose. That's because
he's home alone. Georgie's best friend, Tillie, has
no siblings. Her parents both work till late in the
afternoon. Tillie usually goes to an after-school
program. Sometimes she comes over to our house.
Either way, she doesn't arrive home till after five
o'clock. Igloo has the house to himself *all day*.
Lucky cat.

I think it's time I drop in for a visit.

8.

Igloo's House

I slip in through the upstairs hall window, which has been left open. By the time I reach Igloo, he's awake and lying on his side. He wouldn't be much of a cat if he didn't sense a feline intruder entering his house.

"What's new, Hissy?" he asks.

"Nothing new. Zeb is out of control. Dad broke out the hammers. Listen."

We prick our ears. Despite the distance, the hammering can be heard. Igloo winces.

"Poor you," he says.

"Dad was banging around in his workshop all

day. And not just hammers. Saws, too. And power tools."

"Try to calm down, Hiss. You'll never sleep if you don't relax."

"How can I possibly relax? I don't have a moment's peace!"

A smile spreads across Igloo's snout. I want to smack it off.

"You have a moment right now. Look how the sun is shining on that ottoman. It's all yours."

The sun is shining, bright and golden and warm, on the padded footstool. It looks divine. Tears come to my eyes.

"You are one frazzled feline," Igloo says.

"I know," I say.

"Up you go. Nap time."

I leap onto the ottoman. *Ahhhhhhhhhhh.*

"Sweet dreams," Igloo says.

"Sweet dreams," I answer.

I close my eyes. The closed windows mute the sounds of cars, kids, birds, and dogs. I listen to the sound of my heart beating in my ears. It lulls me. Sweet, sweet slumber, at long last.

I'm on a branch of a tree. There is a warm breeze ruffling my fur. A flock of starlings moves across the sky, like a black cloud. I leap from my branch. I don't know how, but I can fly. I have no wings. I don't flap my legs. I can simply sprint through the air. I sprint after the starlings. I'm so fast! I gain on them easily. The birds are mine for the picking—

"Iggy!" a girl's voice calls. "You're having a playdate! Hi, Hissy!"

Tillie is home.

It must be five o'clock.

How long was I asleep? It seemed like moments.

Tillie rushes up to me. She reaches out a hand, and I hiss. I didn't mean to. It just came out. She backs away.

"Whoa!" Tillie says. "Somebody's waking up on the wrong side of the ottoman!"

"Maybe Hissy should be going home," a woman's voice says. It's Tillie's mom. She waves her arm at the door. "Come on, Hissy. Out you go. Out."

I step down from the warm, comfy ottoman and move groggily toward the door.

"Did somebody leave a window open again?" Tillie's mom asks.

Someone did.

"Sorry, Hiss," Igloo says. "See you later tonight?"

I nod.

Tillie's mom closes the door behind me.

I walk down the front steps in a daze.

A dog gallops up to me. *Woof!* it says. It's Peanut Butter. I coil, flatten my ears, and bare my claws. If he comes any closer, he'll be sorry.

He comes closer.

Hsss-hsss-HSSSSSSSSSS! I say, and swipe at his nose. Dogs' noses are extremely sensitive. He yelps in pain and runs off in the direction from which he came.

He's sorry.

I'm not.

I'm tired of being annoyed.

Everybody had better watch out.

I am Hissy Fitz, and I have had enough.

9.

Looking for Trouble

I'm so dangerous I don't bother climbing trees or buildings. I just walk down the middle of the sidewalk, daring anyone to mess with me. I *hope* someone messes with me.

I walk and walk, not paying much attention to where I'm heading. There's no point in going home. I'll never get any rest there, at least not until the humans go to bed. I feel wild and hungry, like the tigers and lions I've seen on the Fitzes' TV. I'm savage. A predator. A killer. I wouldn't come near me if I were a bird or a mouse. Or a cat or a dog. Or a human.

A group of kids turns the corner and walks toward me. One of them points.

"Look at the blue kitty!" she says.

"Awww, it's so cute!" another says. "Here, kitty! Here, kitty kitty."

As they approach, I give a warning growl. *Grrrrrrrrrr!*

The "here, kitty kitty" girl steps within my striking distance. I scream like a tiger— *RrrOWRRRRRRR!*—and pounce.

The girl screams and leaps backward. A claw catches the lace of her right shoe. She tries to shake herself free, but the claw is stuck.

Hsssssssssss! Hsssssssssss! I say.

"Help!" the girl yells. "Help!"

None of her friends help. They're too terrified. As they should be. The girl kicks her foot and drags me back and forth with it. Which makes me even nastier.

HSSSSSSSSSS! RRROWRRRR! HSSSSSSSSS!

I'm scaring myself.

Finally, my claw comes free. I slash at the girl's foot and catch the lace again. Not so smart, I know, but I can't help it. I'm furious.

The girl screams again. "It's crazy! It won't leave me alone!"

"Kick off your shoe!" one of the other kids says.

The girl pries the shoe off with her other foot, then backs away. I'm left with the shoe. I slide my claw out of the lace, then pull the shoe underneath me and settle down on top of it.

I purr. *Prrrrrrrrrr.*

"It has my shoe!" the girl says.

A boy from the group steps forward and waves his hand at me. "Shoo! Shoo!"

RRROWRRRR! I say, and glare at him with my fiery yellow eyes.

"Leave it alone," another kid says. "Let's just walk away. A cat can't carry a shoe."

Is that so?

If I can carry a rat by the tail, which I can, I can carry a shoe by the lace.

I bite back into it and stand up. The shoe is heavier than a rat, so, instead of carrying it, I drag it away.

"It's stealing my shoe!" the girl says.

"That cat *is* crazy!" the boy says.

After a few strides, however, I tire of dragging the stinky old shoe. I mean, what am I going to do with it? I won this battle. I let it drop, then walk away with my head held high. I don't look back.

10.

Rampage!

I hiss at dogs. Swat at cats. Scream at children. Growl at old people. They call me crazy. Mad. Insane. Wild. And they're right. I'm everybody's worst nightmare, and I will continue to be until everybody gets quiet and lets me sleep.

I wander around the town. I chase squirrels and birds in the parks. I catch a mouse, play with it a while, then eat it. I screech at noisy gulls and sailors at the marina. I hiss at the roaring waves from the rocky beach. I walk down the busy, wide sidewalks of Downtown like I own them.

Some of the people know me.

"Looks like Hissy is on another rampage," one woman says to another.

"Watch out! It's Hissy Fitz! He scratches!" a man says, nudging his wife out of harm's way.

I like it this way. I like being left alone.

Some people, though, don't know me, so I have to show them who's boss of the sidewalk. I growl and glare, and they get out of my way. I give the foolish few who don't a taste of my fury.

HSSSSSSSSSS! RRROWRRRR! GRRRRRRRRRR!

I don't mind having to teach them to respect me.

None of this helps me with my problem, of course. Quite the opposite. The more upset I get, the less likely it is that I'll be able to sleep. In addition, this exercise makes me hungry and thirsty.

I head for the Dumpsters.

There are rows of big garbage bins behind all the restaurants Downtown. And there are quite a few restaurants. And many of those restaurants serve fish. And some of that perfectly good fish gets thrown away. Not all of the Dumpsters are open, though, and the lids are too heavy for a cat to budge. I find one open behind the Salty Cod and dive in. I come out with a chunk of salmon in my mouth. I duck under some bushes and wolf it down. Real salmon sure beats Salmon Supper.

As I often do on these adventures, I start thinking about giving up being a house cat. I think about going wild. Feral. About living outside full time.

But I know I can't. For one thing, most cats that go wild don't live long. There are too many perils. Cars. Truly wild animals, like coyotes and raccoons. I'm out on a limb here, roaming the town, acting as if nothing can hurt me.

And then there are the Fitzes. True, they drive me crazy. But Abe and Mom are kind to me. Dad makes a terrible racket, but he means well. And Georgie . . . well, she needs me, of course. She'd be heartbroken if I left. I guess I would be, too.

Zeb I could live without.

The sun is now low in the sky. Mom is probably home. She has a way of calming Zeb down. Before long it will be the humans' bedtimes, and the house will finally quiet down. Maybe, after a hectic day like this, I'll actually be able to sleep. I'm not counting on it, but it could happen.

I clean myself up after my snack, then head back through town. The food has soothed my rage somewhat, though I still hiss and scream and swat at passersby. I stop for a drink at the city fountain with the statue of the mermaid in the center. A sparrow foolishly lands beside me and pecks at the water. My killer instinct kicks in, but I don't give into it. I let the bird live. It doesn't know how lucky it is that I'm fed.

I jump down from the fountain to start the long walk home. I climb the 126 stairs leading up from the fountain to our neighborhood, which the people call Uptown. By the time I hit the top step I'm hungry again and regret letting the sparrow go.

I hope someone has refilled my food dish. If not, someone is going to pay.

11.

swagger

Before the flap to my
door slaps shut behind
me, Zeb is there.
"Hissy cat!"
he hollers, and
attempts to grab
my tail.
I give him my leopard
impression: fangs bared,
back arched, hackles up,
eyes wild, my loudest
scream. *RRROWWWRRRR!*

Zeb backs off, but I don't. I launch at him, all four paws off the ground, all eighteen of my claws bared. I'm not messing around.

Zeb's face turns white. He twists to run, gets tangled up on his own feet, and falls to the floor. I land beside him. I could pounce on him, teach him a lesson. I should.

But I don't. He's only a child. I merely scold him: *Hsssssssss!*

"Mama!" he cries. "Maaaaa-maaaaa!" He scrambles to his feet and flees.

That was enjoyable.

I stroll over to my dishes. No food. No water.

Grrrrrrrrrr!

Never mind. I smell something more delicious. There's a bag of groceries on the counter. I leap up onto it. The smell is bird. It's in the bag. I slash through the paper, then paw through the people food inside: apples, oranges, carrots, cabbage, a couple boxes of pasta, some cans of beans and then . . . a chicken breast! I slash through the plastic wrap into the bird's flesh. Blood stains my claws. I lick them clean. I slash again.

"Hissy!" Mom says.

I jump. Didn't hear her come in. Too focused on the poultry.

She's already changed out of her business clothes. She's in yoga pants and a sweatshirt.

"Get down!" she says, walking briskly toward me.

Hssssssssss! I say.

I like Mom, but I don't like being told what to do.

"Go on," she says, waving her hand at me. "Get down. Get down!"

I hiss louder. *HSSSSSSSSSS!*

"Don't you have any food of your own?" She checks my dishes. "You don't. And no water, either. Georgie!"

Good. She sees the problem here. I respect Mom's good sense. I jump down.

But Georgie doesn't appear. A violin is screeching in the living room. Georgie is learning to play the foul instrument. Of the many earsplitting things humans have invented, the violin must be the worst. As Georgie saws on hers, she also sings along. She makes up the words as she goes.

"Where are my SLIP-pers!

They're right UN-der the chair, said her mother,

They're right O-ver here, said her father,

They are right . . . here."

It's doubtful Georgie can hear her mother over the din she is making.

"*Georgie!*" Mom calls her again in a louder, shriller voice. I wince. Then she starts putting away the groceries.

"Zeb says you attacked him," she says to me.

True, but Zeb had it coming.

"I'm sure he deserved it," she adds.

Absolutely.

"I'd feed you myself, but I want Georgie to do it. It's her job."

I understand—so long as I get fed and watered.

She yells her daughter's name again even louder, even shriller, at the exact moment Georgie appears in the doorway.

"Here I am!" she chirps.

"Did you forget to feed Hissy?"

"No, I fed him when I got home," Georgie says. "He must have eaten it all. Is he still hungry?"

He is.

"He just tore into the groceries," Mom says.

"Should I feed him again?"

Yes.

"Did you give him wet food?"

"Yes," Georgie says.

"Then just give him a little dry. We don't want him getting fat."

Grrrrrrrrr.

"And water, too," Mom says. "Better do it quickly. He's been hissing at me. And he attacked Zeb."

"Zeb probably deserved it," Georgie says with a roll of her eyes.

Georgie scoops some kibbles out of the bag and pours them into my dish. They make an unappetizing tinkling sound.

I eat a couple. Compared to the salmon in the

Dumpster, kibbles taste like dirt. I gulp them down, lap up some water, then stroll away.

"That's all you want?" Mom asks. "After all that fuss?"

The fuss, I wish I could tell her, is not about food and drink. It is about sleep. It is about not being able to get any in this house. Since I can't tell her, I lift my tail and add a little swagger to my walk.

12.

The Bug

I hurry up to the parents' bedroom and scoot under their big bed. It's the family's dinnertime, and I'm hoping to get in a quick nap while they're all busy eating.

I tuck my legs under me and shut my eyes. All the muscles in my body instantly relax. I feel as if I'm melting.

I am a lion, dozing on the savannah. Gazelles and zebras circle around me, but I am too bushed to lift my enormous, maned head. I'm too tired to hunt.

"Hissy!" Georgie says. "Hissy Fitz! Come out of there!"

I open my eyes. She's peeking under the bed at me.

"Hurry, before Zeb gets here!"

The light in the hall is shining in my eyes. It wasn't on when I came up here. Georgie must have turned it on. But why would she? Night hasn't fallen yet.

Or has it?

"He's still at the table. Mama won't let him get up till he eats a vegetable. Come on! We can play in my room."

I don't want to play in her room. I want to—

What's that? Something is swishing back and forth in front of me.

It disappeared!

It's back!

Georgie giggles. "What do you see, Hissy? What is it? Come and see, Hissy. Come on. Come out and see what it is."

It acts like a bug. It flutters. It zigzags. I grip the carpet with my claws and prepare to pounce.

I'm not fooled, of course. Georgie's trying to lure me out with a cat toy, a wad of paper tied to a wire. I'm not going to—

There it is again! To the right. It's on the move. I must catch it before it gets away.

I creep forward.

"That's it, Hissy," Georgie says. "Get it. Go on. . . ."

My movements are smooth and silent. I'm practically gliding across the rug. The bug/toy dances a herky-jerky jig. Then it flies straight up, out of sight. I must get out from under the bed!

"Where'd it go, Hissy? Where'd it go? It flew away, I think. It's gone, Hissy. You didn't catch it."

I stick my nose out from under the bed and glance upward. I don't see the bug. But I hear a dull thumping on the bedspread.

"It's on the bed, Hissy! It's on the bed! Get it, Hissy! Get it!"

I run out from under the bed and look back to see the bug flopping on it. There's no time to lose! I spring onto the bed—which is taller than the kids'—just as the bug lifts off. It disappears again. Rats!

"Oh, no," Georgie says, pretending to be disappointed. "I guess it really did get away this—no, *there* it is!" The bug flies back and flitters in circles right over my head. I swat at it and miss. Georgie laughs. I spin around and swat again. I miss again. Georgie laughs harder.

"You can get it, Hissy! Don't give up!"

She continues to make the thing dance in the air. I want to teach Georgie a lesson for waking me. I will catch it and rip it to shreds before her eyes. Then we'll see who laughs best.

I leap into the air, but she jerks the toy away in the nick of time. She lifts it higher. I leap higher. She jerks it away. I land awkwardly and fall on my side. She laughs. I spring to my feet.

Hsssssssss! I say.

"Oh, don't get mad, Hissy. Keep trying. You'll get it."

I lunge at the wire and catch it with my right paw. My claw slides along the wire, pulling the toy downward, where I can reach it. The "bug" is a twisted pipe cleaner. I feverishly claw at it. I bite it. I growl. I win.

"You got it!" Georgie squeals. "Good boy, Hissy! Good boy! Now let go and we'll do it again."

I let go. She hovers it over my head again. I yawn. There will be no rematch.

I walk across the bedspread to the edge and jump down. Through the window I see it is dark outside. I guess I did fall asleep.

The nap was too short to help, though. And I spent what little energy I had saved chasing after Georgie's toy. Soon Zeb will be on the loose again.

It may be dark, but the human day has not yet ended.

13.

Bath Time

I hide in the pantry during bath time, behind the cans. Zeb and Abe bathe first. The only voice I hear is Zeb's. He is imitating the sounds of motors and weapons. Revving sounds. Machine-gun fire. Explosions. There are also the sounds of splashing and tussling. It is a scene to avoid.

Just as I'm drifting off, Georgie steps into the pantry.

She sits cross-legged on the other side of the cans.

"I can't believe that Ethan lets Peanut Butter run around without a leash like that," she says. "Then he gets mad at poor Zeb for chasing him. It's not Zeb's fault. If Peanut Butter was on a leash, Zeb wouldn't chase him."

No, he would just torment him. Maybe try to ride him. He's done that to dogs before.

"Did you see Peanut Butter lick my face? He has such a big tongue!" She sticks hers out in disgust. "But it's not his fault. He should be on a leash."

I agree with her, though I wouldn't like to be leashed. Cats are lucky that way. We can go where we want. Most of us, anyway. I know cats who are kept inside. Igloo, for example. Their owners don't want them to get run over by cars, or get into fights with other cats, or catch diseases, or kill birds. Igloo's family tries to keep him inside, but he always escapes. I'm glad my humans don't try to keep me inside. I'd go crazy locked up in this house.

Not that I don't feel crazy now. I must get some rest.

I hate to do it, but I'm going to have to . . .

Hssssssssss!

"Hissy! What's the matter?"

I rise up, arch my back, repeat myself. *Hsssssssss!* Then, to be sure I get my point across, I spit: *Fffft! Fffft!*

She inches away.

"Is it because I'm talking about Peanut Butter? Is that why you're so upset?"

She's not getting it. I want to be left alone.

Hsssssssss! Fffft! Fffft!

She reaches out a hand, as if to pet me.

I swat at it, and, again, say, *HSSSSSSSSS!*

I won't lie. It feels good. Besides, it's not as if I have the option of politely asking her for some privacy.

"Georgie!" Mom's voice calls. "Bath time!"

"I have to go take my bath," Georgie says to me, climbing to her feet. "Let's talk about this later."

Hsssssssss!

She scoots out the door.

I close my eyes. All the hissing has made my heart race. It will take a while before I can calm down enough to sleep.

Feet pound on the stairs overhead. The pantry is under the staircase.

"Hissy cat!" I hear. "Where are you?"

"Zeb!" Mom yells. "You're soaking wet! Get back here!"

"Hissy cat! I'll find yoooooooou!"

Oh, help.

14.

Very Mad Cat

The footsteps I hear in the kitchen are light and slow. They're not Zeb's.

Abe slips into the pantry, quiet as a mouse. Clearly, he's trying not to be seen by his brother.

Though I'd prefer being alone, I'm relieved. I don't have to worry about Abe talking my ear off, as Georgie does, or pulling my ear off, as Zeb tries to do. Abe sits on the floor and sets Medium Sad Guy in his lap. His face is flush from the bath and his hair is mussed from the towel drying. He's wearing his pajamas. He smells like apricots.

He sits a while without saying a word. It's soothing, his silence. My eyelids close on their own. I breathe deeply. I feel safe, as if I had a protector. Then Abe moves, and my eyes open. He's lifting Medium Sad Guy to his ear. He "listens" to it, nods, then sets it back in his lap. He does this with such seriousness that I begin to wonder if somehow the stuffed-rabbit puppet really does speak to him.

I'm getting loopy. I *desperately* need sleep.

I close my eyes.

"Medium Sad Guy says good night, Hissy. And sweet dreams."

I open my eyes, halfway. The boy is looking at me, his hazel eyes wide, his mouth puckered. For a human, he's pretty adorable.

I'm sliding my eyelids closed again when Abe brings the puppet back up to his ear. He listens. He lowers the puppet. I wait for him to relay the message.

He says nothing. I guess Medium Sad Guy had nothing further to say to me. His message was for Abe alone.

So I close my eyes.

"Medium Sad Guy told me I should say good night and sweet dreams to you, too," Abe says. "Good night, Hissy. Sweet dreams."

I open one eye, halfway. I love the kid. I don't want to have to hiss at him. So I glare at him. I'm telling him with my half eye that he needs to stop talking. Then I lower the eyelid the rest of the way.

He says nothing more. There is silence in the house. I have no idea why Zeb isn't making noise, but he isn't. I enjoy this little miracle.

I don't fall asleep, though. I keep expecting another message from the rabbit. I try to put it out my mind, try to relax, try to drift off. But I'm afraid the second I let myself drop off, Abe will lift the puppet to his ear again.

I open an eye a crack and peek at him. He's inspecting Medium Sad Guy's fur the way his mom inspects his hair for lice. Or me for fleas. I close my eye. Maybe there's nothing to worry about.

The door bursts open.

"BOO!" Zeb shouts, leaping into the room, wrapped in a towel. "Snuck up on you! Ha!"

HSSSSSSSSSS! I say, and fly over the cans. Or part
of the way over the cans. I accidentally kick them
with my hind paws, and they topple with a clatter.
Abe leaps to his feet and hits his head on a shelf,
which causes a bag of flour to fall. It explodes
on the floor in a white cloud. I dive through it
toward the door.

I'm hissing, snarling, spitting, and swatting as I pass Zeb. One of my claws catches his towel and I end up dragging it into the kitchen. I stop and, in a fury, shake it off. Then I fly up the stairs to the parents' room and dive under their bed. I start cleaning the flour from my fur.

I hear calling and pounding of feet as Mom and Dad run to find out what happened, then more calling and pounding as they try to catch Zeb.

Georgie joins in the chase. She's angry that Zeb's been chasing me again and is scolding him loudly. I don't hear a peep from Abe. I hope he didn't hurt his head badly.

My heart is pounding like one of Dad's hammers. Will this family ever stop tormenting me? Will they ever let me sleep?

Maybe now's the time. They're all busy. And the kids' bedtime comes next, so the parents won't be coming in here for a while. If I can tune out the noise, maybe I can doze off.

"Zeb! Come here and put some clothes on!" Mom says.

"Zeb! Stop chasing Hissy!" Georgie says.

"Zeb! Come down off that ladder!" Dad says.

I doubt I can tune out the noise.

Besides, night has fallen, and the hunting instinct has switched on. It's as if a light has been turned on inside me, and it's shining out through my eyes. I feel the urge to go outside, to go hunting. It's not something I want to do, or need to do. It's something I *am*.

It's time for the cat to go out.

15.

Savage Predator

The night air is chilled. Through the trees, the sky twinkles with stars. I feel energy surge within me. The night is where I belong. I feel alive.

The humans say the night is dark, but not to a cat. I don't see darkness. The world is always bright, just a little less so at night.

I move along from branch to fence to roof, every step made softly and surely. My tail shifts angles to keep me balanced. The breeze whiffles my fur. What a fine thing it is to be a cat in the nighttime!

"Hissy!" a feline voice calls. "Hissy Fitz! Who are you running from?"

It's Igloo, sitting on the slanted roof of his house. His white coat seems to glow in the starlight.

"No one. I'm just running. How'd you get out this time?"

"They forgot to lock my cat door. Did you finally get a nap?"

I give him a look.

He laughs. "You do have a noisy family."

"You don't know how lucky you are, having only Tillie to deal with."

"At least you have your freedom," Igloo says.

True. I can escape.

"Why don't you come and have a nap with me?" Igloo asks.

"Later. I need to prowl a while first."

"Can I come along?"

I prefer to prowl alone, but tonight I wouldn't mind having someone to talk to. To complain to. Maybe if I talk about my problems, I'll be able to relax.

"Sure," I say. "But you have to keep up."

Igloo's a longhair. The fur on his belly grazes the ground when he walks. It's often snarled and littered with debris. It slows him down. I'm glad I'm a shorthair. A British shorthair, to be exact.

I move on. Igloo runs after me.

"How was your day after you left my house?" he asks.

"Frustrating," I say, and tell him about my afternoon: about the shoelace, Zeb trying to grab my tail, Georgie's bug, Medium Sad Guy, Zeb scaring Abe and me to death.

"That does sound frustrating," Igloo says. "But it's over now. There's no point in—"

"You don't know what it's like," I interrupt. "You get to sleep all day. Missing a day of sleep makes me crazy. And then they all go to bed, and I'm supposed to drop off. It isn't easy. I mean, it's *night*. And I'm all wound up."

"You need to let it go, Hiss. You'll never get to sleep."

If he doesn't stop talking about how I need to relax, I'm going to swat him. I know I need to relax. I know I need to let it go. But I've got a fire in my belly, and in my brain. That's why I'm prowling. Sometimes exercise cools the flames.

"Keep up!" I say with a hiss. He's lagging behind.

"I'm trying," Igloo says, "but you're moving pretty fast."

"Then don't keep up! Go back to your roof and sleep!"

"Hissy, try to calm—"

Hssssssssss! I say, whirling around on him. I lash out. He recoils in fear.

"Take it easy—"

I swat at him again and scream, *RrrOWRRRR!*

"Okay, okay, I'm going," he says with a light laugh. He turns away. "But you really do need to chill—"

RrrOWRRRR!

He chuckles. "Come by when you're ready to nap. I'll be on my roof."

We part ways. I leave the family and my friend behind. I'm too dangerous to be around anyone. Too wild. Too savage. I'm a savage predator, gliding through the town's canopy, like a panther.

RrrOWRRRR!

I feel alive.

16.

Sea Sid

There are fewer trees as I near the marina. Soon
there are no treetops to glide through. I drop to the
ground and slink around under bushes and cars.

At the docks, the boats rock lightly in the dark
water, their bare masts swaying.

"Hissy," a voice says. "Hissy Fitz. What are you
doing here? And at this hour? Shouldn't you be
home, snug at the foot of your owner's bed?"

It's Sid. She's a sleek black cat that lives on
the waterfront. She's not feral; she has tags. A
fisherman bought them for her so she wouldn't
be thrown into an animal shelter. She lives on

his boat, but says she doesn't belong to him. She
doesn't belong to anyone but herself.

I don't answer any of her questions because
I don't think they're really questions.
They're comments. She looks
down on house cats.

"Hi, Sid. Where's your fisherman?"

"Asleep in his cabin."

"Did he bring you home any fish?"

She lifts an eyebrow. "I don't have a home.
But yeah, he tossed me a snack when he came in.

We're friends. I keep rats out of his boat. He tosses me fish."

"Any left?"

"Nope."

That's too bad. Prowling makes a cat hungry.

"So what's up, Hissy? Can't sleep again?" She gives a snort.

I give a growl.

"Take it easy, Hiss. Come out onto the boat. It'll rock you to sleep."

It's worth a try, though I do still feel pretty wound up. Being mocked by Sid doesn't help.

"It's worth a try," I say. "Lead the way."

We walk the dock till we come to a fishing boat named *Louise*. The word is painted on the hull. Sid leaps aboard, and I follow. We settle down on the bow. Sid stretches, then curls up. I do the same. She closes her eyes; I close mine.

My fatigue catches up with me. Boy, I'm tired. Bone-tired. Wiped. My eyelids are as heavy as lead. A warm tingle washes over me. This is it. Aside from the creaking of the dock, the lapping of the waves, the occasional donging of a bell on a buoy, it is quiet. Time for a nap.

My stomach, however, begs to differ. It's upset. It tightens. Turns. I may be sick.

I'm definitely going to be sick.

Yeowwwwwwww! I say, and leap to the dock.

"What's the matter, Hiss?" Sid laughs. "Seasick?"

Hsssssssss! I answer.

She laughs again.

It's not funny.

"I guess that comfy bed back home doesn't rock," Sid says.

The dock does, though. My stomach is churning. I run back along it.

"Adios, landlubber!" Sid calls after me.

A landlubber is someone who doesn't sail on the sea. Sid has called me—and Igloo, and other cats—that name before.

"Adios, sea dog!" I call back from dry land. A sea dog is an experienced sailor. I know she doesn't like the name.

"Sea *cat*!" she yells.

17.

Clumsy Quiche

I make my way downtown. Walking on solid
ground soothes my sour stomach. A few restaurants
are open. People walk in and out. I climb a tree that
grows out of a perfectly round circle in the sidewalk
to the roof of a one-story building. From there I
climb a fire escape to the third floor of an old brick
building. I leap to a windowsill. The window is
open.

This is Quiche's apartment. He lives alone
with an old man named Gary Rodriguez. The man
speaks to Quiche in English, but scolds him in

Spanish. At this hour, the man will be asleep. He's an early-to-bed, early-to-rise sort of human.

I mew, and instantly hear the padding of cat paws.

Quiche, a black-and-white tabby with a black jaw that looks like a beard, enters the room and leaps up onto a table beneath the window. He knocks over an empty vase. The sound makes us both flinch. Quiche is one clumsy cat.

"Hi, Hissy," he says. "You can't sleep?"

Why does that question always raise my hackles? I should be glad that my friends know me so well. Quiche is a genuinely kind cat. I'm sure he asks only because he cares about me. Still, I growl, then answer in a testy voice, "Obviously."

"I'd invite you in, but Mr. Rodriguez is up. He can't sleep, either."

"Insomnia," I say.

"Right. He's reading in his chair."

"Want to come out and do some prowling? Find something to eat?"

"I shouldn't leave. Mr. Rodriguez likes company

when he can't sleep. I was sitting in his lap when
you mewed. Besides, I just ate."

Everything is annoying me. It's no wonder. I'm
absolutely exhausted. Wired. Edgy. Touchy.

Grrrrrrrrrr!

"I'm awfully sorry, Hiss."

I snarl, then turn to leave.

"When the old guy goes to sleep, I'll come find
you."

"I'll be Dumpster diving," I grunt over my
shoulder.

I pad down the fire escape, retrace my steps back
to the sidewalk, then make my way toward the
Dumpsters. Even before I reach them, I sense that
someone has beaten me to it.

18.

Clumsy Raccoon

There is the scrabbling of claws and a familiar light chattering sound. It's a raccoon.

I normally steer clear of them. They look somewhat cute and cuddly, yet they're anything but. They're vile and vicious. I'm feeling fairly vile and vicious myself at the moment, so I bound up a board that is leaning against one of the Dumpsters. The raccoon isn't inside, so I dive in and start pawing through the garbage. I find some cooked chicken, part of a burger, some trout, and plenty of vegetables, which I ignore. As if I'd eat a potato! I start with the chicken. I had fish already today. The beef will be dessert.

That's when I hear the raccoon walking up the board. *Ticka-ticka-ticka-ticka-ticka-tick!* the beast says when it reaches the top and looks down at me. This is a raccoon's warning sound, and, frankly, it's sad. It reminds me of the sound Georgie's bike wheel makes when she puts a playing card in her spokes. Not scary.

HSSSSSSSSSS! I say, baring my fangs, flattening my little ears. I throw in some spitting for good measure: *Ffft! Ffft!*

I don't like that the raccoon is above me. Cats like being above. We like to plunge down onto our prey, and onto our foes. But my mood is so foul, I don't think it will matter. Nothing is nastier than I am tonight.

The raccoon keeps ticking, so I give a panther cry: *RrrrOWWWRRRRRRRRRRRR!*

It's one terrifying cry, if I do say so myself. I'd be terrified of me.

The raccoon stops ticking, but doesn't back down.

This makes me even angrier, which I didn't realize was possible. *RrrrOWWWRRRRRRRRRRRR!* I cry again, then fly at the disrespectful beast. My aim is short, however; I hit the metal wall of the Dumpster with a loud *CLANG!* The clumsy raccoon loses its balance and falls into the garbage with me.

This is what Zeb would call a "cage match." Two foes, locked in a closed space, go to battle. Many times has Zeb slammed a closet or bathroom door behind us and yelled the words, "Cage match!" With Zeb, I scream and swipe at him till he opens the door. Once I had to draw a little blood. With Zeb, a little is enough.

I'm willing to go further with the raccoon.

It hunkers down in the garbage and growls. It's a deep, snorty growl, like a hog's, interrupted by forceful puffs of air through its nose. Meanwhile, it pumps itself up and down with its forelegs, like it's doing push-ups. What a goofy creature.

I likewise crouch, tightening my hind legs for another powerful launch. Hopefully, this one will be better aimed. No, it *will* be better aimed. And when I land on the clumsy, goofy, ticking animal, with my eighteen razor-sharp claws slashing, it will learn that I deserve respect.

HSSSSSSSSSS! I say. I feel strong and fierce and very, very, *very* awake. I am a cat in the nighttime, and this raccoon doesn't stand a—

He pounces.

19.

Panther
of the Night

The masked intruder is on top of me, but only for a moment. I whirl and let loose a flurry of swats and kicks.

A sudden sharp pain in my left ear causes me to fly into a frenzy. I scream, scratch, spit, snap. We tangle, rolling around in the garbage, banging into the metal walls. The raccoon has a thick pelt, but my claws are hooked knives, and they pierce through it. The animal yelps and pushes itself away. I slash its striped tail as it retreats. It yelps again.

A rapid chirping now comes from the wounded creature. It wanders around the Dumpster, its nose up in the air. It's finished fighting. It's looking for a way out. I've won. Huzzah!

Raccoons are excellent climbers, but they can't jump. They're too fat and squat. This raccoon let its nose lead it into a trap. It peeked into the Dumpster to see what was inside, and now it's inside and can't get out. Curiosity killed the raccoon? *Heh.*

Still, somehow I feel sorry for the beast. It's small. I doubt it's an adult. Still a child. Like Zeb, or Georgie. Maybe that's why it was so easy to defeat. Maybe I should let it be. I've won the battle. I've had my snack. I have my battle scar. Time to move on.

I give the raccoon one last hiss, then spring easily to the Dumpster's rim. I perch there a moment, smiling down at the marooned animal. I'm sure a human will hear its chirping and release it. In time. While it waits, it can think about the mistakes it's made, including the damage it did to the ear of Hissy Fitz, Panther of the Night.

I jump onto the closed lid of the neighboring Dumpster, then to the fence that encloses the bunch of them. From there I scramble up the trunk of a tree to a branch, to the ledge of a building, to a low roof, to a taller one, and on like this, making my way across Downtown.

I stop sometimes to groom and tend to my wound. I must keep it clean. I've made too many trips to the animal hospital. I don't like it there. It's filled with whining, whimpering pets, all ill or injured. Some are birds and rodents, which is nerve-racking. With prey all around me, I'm locked in a tiny kennel. The vet prods and pokes me and even stabs me with a needle. Humans have odd ideas about healing. I prefer just to lick my wounds.

As I near the humans' sports field, I hear familiar voices. Cat voices. I'd guess there are more than ten of them. I can make out three: Igloo, Sid, and Quiche. Why are they all together? And why here?

I can't see what's going on inside, as the field is surrounded by a wood-slat fence that begins and ends at a set of concrete bleachers, so I scale the fence and perch atop it.

What I find is surprising. Even shocking. And absolutely ridiculous.

20.

Cat Teams

There are cats on the field. I can't tell how many, as they're milling about in a group. My guess would be there are a dozen or so. Many of their tails point upward. An upward-pointing tail is a sign of a happy cat. I would not expect a group of cats to be happy.

Cats don't hang out in groups. Is there even a word for a group of cats? Dogs hang in packs, birds in flocks, but the house cat, like the panther and the tiger, is a solitary creature. Seeing so many together without their fur flying is strange.

Among them is a ball with a pattern of black and white shapes. The cats are playing soccer.

They can't kick the ball, of course. It's too big, and their paws are too small. They bump and push it with their heads. A pair of teammates sometimes run at the ball together, for more impact. Opposing pairs run at it from the opposite direction. The result is often cats sprawled in the grass around the ball, which hasn't budged. The players laugh, then spring back to their feet and lunge at the ball again.

I jump down from the fence and walk out onto the field.

"Igloo!" I call. "Have you gone crazy?"

"Hissy Fitz!" he answers, lifting his head above the fray. "We've been hoping you'd show up!"

"Time out!" Sid yells.

The scrimmage pauses.

"You're on my team," Sid says. "I'm the captain of the shorthairs. It's a close game. Zero to zero. But we're outnumbered, six to five. We could use you."

"I don't understand what's going on," I say. "Why on earth are you playing *soccer*? You're cats! Cats aren't ballplayers. Cats aren't *team* players."

"Maybe, but it's working," Igloo says with a smile.

The rest of the cats smile in agreement. It's weird to see eleven cats standing together, smiling.

I recognize a few of them: Martin, the ash-colored calico that lives a few blocks from us; Teacup, the elegant Balinese from the condos by the park; Schmookie, the longhair calico with tiger stripes; and some others I've seen around but whose names I don't know, or have forgotten.

"It was my idea," Igloo says. "After you left my house, I got to thinking how tired you were, and how much trouble you were having getting to sleep at night. I wanted to help somehow. I thought maybe a game would take your mind off the terrible day you've had and would tire you out in the process. So I rounded everyone up. I pushed the soccer ball here myself."

"All the way?"

"Well, it's mostly downhill."

"You did this for me?" I ask.

"I did. But we're having fun, so it ended up being for everyone."

The cats all smile again.

"How did you get them to come?"

"I just told them to meet me here, that something unusual was going to happen. I let feline curiosity do the rest. I looked but couldn't find you."

"I had a cage match with a raccoon. In a Dumpster."

The group gasps.

"I won," I say, "though the beast did slice my ear." I tilt my head so they can see the slice.

Another gasp.

I puff out my chest.

"So come on, Hiss," Sid says, nudging me with her shoulder. "That's our goal line over there."

She points to the north end of the field. There are no goals on the field, just lines in the grass.

"So what do you say, Hiss?" Igloo asks. "You in?"

It seems so silly, cats playing soccer, but I am . . . well . . . curious.

"I'm in."

21.

Halftime

I learn quickly that head butting a soccer ball
doesn't move it very far. Pouncing on it, sinking
your claws into it, then pushing off with your hind
paws is much more effective.

It's not as simple as it sounds. For one thing, it
isn't easy to land on a ball without making it roll
the wrong way. One needs to land on the ball in
the opposite direction from the one you want it
to go. Doing so takes great balance, control, and
timing. Fortunately, I have great balance, control,
and timing.

The other cats see that I've figured out a better way to move the ball, and before long they're all pouncing on it, too. This results in many rather comical midair collisions. The crashes are so amusing that instead of leading to catfights, they lead to laughter and upward-pointing tails.

The ball rolls one way across the field, then rolls back. Not much ground is made by either team. One might think we'd weary of this pretty quickly, but we don't. Cats love chasing a ball around.

Every once in a while, though, one of us gets tired and yowls, "Time out!" We all immediately collapse onto the grass. The second any cat snoozes, though, Sid wakes everyone up with a loud "Time in!" and the game resumes.

At some point, Teacup calls "Time out!" then asks, "Anyone hungry?"

We all are, so Sid calls, "Halftime! Find something to eat. You have twenty minutes."

I can't resist the temptation to return to the Dumpster where the raccoon is trapped. Igloo, Teacup, and Martin follow along.

The raccoon is still in the garbage bin. It whines as we crouch on the rim, looking down at it.

"You were down there with *that*?" Martin asks.

I nod. This time I don't puff out my chest, though. I suddenly feel bad for the poor thing.

The board is still leaning against the Dumpster. It's a long plank, and it gives me an idea.

"Igloo, help me out, will you?"

"Sure," he says.

"You and a couple of cats walk down the plank and sit on it at the bottom."

"Sit on it? Why?"

"You'll see."

He smiles. "Okay, Hiss." He walks down the plank. Teacup and Martin follow him.

"Now stay seated till I tell you to jump off," I say.

I step onto the plank, but instead of climbing down, I climb up. The board bows slightly from my weight. I creep to the end.

The raccoon watches me from below. *Ticka-ticka-ticka-ticka-tick*, it says.

"You ready, Igloo?" I ask.

"Ready!"

"On the count of three. One . . . two . . . *three!*"

The cats leap from their end of the board, and my end plummets toward the garbage, toward the raccoon. It squeals and runs for a corner. A split second before the plank hits the Dumpster floor, I spring from it, landing back up on the bin's rim. The plank clatters below me.

Igloo and the other cats join me on the rim.

"You've given the raccoon a ramp to freedom," Igloo says.

I nod.

Teacup shivers, then jumps down and scurries away.

"I guess she didn't want to see the raccoon climb to freedom," Igloo laughed.

"I doubt it will climb out with us up here," I say. "Let's give it some space. Once it's out, we'll get some food, then get back to the game."

"You're a good cat, Hissy Fitz," Igloo says.

"I wouldn't say that."

But it's nice that he did.

22.

The Champions

Once we've eaten and found some water—from a leaky sprinkler—we return to the field. The others are all there, lying in the grass, grooming.

"Are we ready to start again?" Igloo asks.

No one answers. The food has slowed us down. Personally, some shut-eye sounds like a great idea.

"No?" Igloo laughs. "Okay. Why don't we take a short catnap. Wake us up in a bit, okay, Sid?"

Sid is curled up with her head on her paws. "Sure," she says drowsily.

Before long we all are curled up with our heads on our paws. One by one, we shut our eyes.

I run down the field, kicking the ball with my hind paws. I'm running upright, like a human, as are the other cats. I approach the goal—and there is an actual goal now, with a net—and give a swift, hard kick. Sid lunges to block it. I think, *Wait, she's on my team,* but dreams never make sense. The ball is beyond her reach and sinks into the netting. Score!

The crowd roars. Yes, there's a crowd. My teammates hoist me up onto their shoulders and carry me around the field. We won the game. We are the champion soccer cats of the world!

"We are the champions!" we chant. "We are the champions!"

"Hissy?" Sid says. Her face is right over mine. Stars are twinkling behind it. "You're shouting."

I lift my head. The other cats are lying on the grass, glaring at me. I guess I woke them.

"Sorry," I say. "I was dreaming."

"That's okay," says Sid. "Since we're all awake, let's get back to the game."

The others grumble, but slowly rise to their feet,

stretching and arching their backs. I'm still on the ground.

"Come on, Hiss," Sid says, nudging me.

The sleep felt good. I need more of it.

"Leave me alone. I want to sleep."

She nudges me again. "We need you, Hiss. You're the best pouncer on our team."

She's right, of course.

"Oh, all right."

I'm such a pushover.

I climb to my feet and stretch.

"What's the score?" Martin asks.

We all laugh.

"Still tied," Igloo says. "Zero to zero."

"Play ball!" Sid cries.

23.

Before
the Madness

The second half is much like the first. Plenty of leaping and head butting, but very little ball movement. As the night wears on, we grow tired and testy. We growl and snarl and swat more. Especially me. This has been a fun distraction from my problem, but it is still there: I need sleep.

Wait. It's the middle of the night. There are no sounds of hammers or lawn mowers. There are few automobiles on the roads. No garbage trucks, no school buses. It's quiet. The humans are in their beds all over town.

The hunting instinct isn't as strong now. Maybe it's because I've worn myself out playing this game. I've exhausted all desires. I'm beyond bone-tired. I'm brain-tired. Heart-tired. Skin-tired. Paw-tired. I'm tired from the tip of my sliced ear to the tip of my ringed tail.

I walk away from the scuffle.

"Hissy!" Sid yells. "What are you doing? Where are you going? The game's not over. It's still tied. We need you!"

"Maybe you do," I say, "but I need some sleep. I'm heading home."

"I need sleep, too," says Schmookie.

"Me, too," Quiche says.

Pretty soon everyone, including Sid, has quit the game.

"We'll call it a tie," she says with a yawn.

We all nod, then walk away toward our homes—or, in Sid's case, toward her boat.

"Wait up, Hiss," Igloo says, running after me. "That was fun, right?"

"It was," I say. "Thanks."

"My pleasure. I hope you can get some sleep before the family starts waking up."

I think about this. Zeb is usually up first, and once he is, the whole house is up, including me. Then comes the getting ready for school and work. Zeb always refuses to cooperate. He makes a big fuss, tearing around the house, yelling.

"I hope so, too," I say.

24.

Awake
in a Dream

I hear the clock in the living room ticking. I hear
the little snorts Dad makes when he sleeps. I
hear my paws on the linoleum. That's how quiet
it is in the house.

I glide through the kitchen and up the stairs
to Georgie's room. She's on her bed, out cold,
her arms and legs pointing in odd directions. Her
blanket and sheet are in a knot. She tosses and
turns when she sleeps, which can be challenging. I
don't want to be wakened by an elbow or a flying
kick. I consider moving to her little stuffed chair,
but I want Georgie's warmth. I want her next to
me. It makes no sense, but I miss her.

I leap onto the bed and nestle in beside her. She's on her side, breathing softly, her belly rising and falling against me. She's warm indeed. I purr. *Prrrrrrrrrr.*

I believe there are a few precious hours left before the dawn. Zeb usually sleeps till the sun comes up, but there's no telling what will happen when it comes to Zebediah Irwin Fitz. As splendid as it is lying here, enjoying the silence and Georgie's warmth, I close my eyes.

I am a lion perched on a mountain ledge, looking down over a green valley. A herd of hoofed, antlered animals graze below. Gazelles? I can't tell from this distance. My stomach growls, but I am too tired to move. I roar. *RrrOWRRRR!* The animals stop eating and lift their heads in unison. Then they begin to run away. They move left, then right, then left, as if they were one creature. I watch until I can't keep my eyelids open any longer. They slide shut.

"Hissy cat!" Zeb screams.

My eyes open. He is looming over me, a villainous grin on his face. In his hand, raised over his head, is a hammer.

Hsssssssss! I say, and jump back. My eyes open, for real this time, and I find myself on Georgie's bed. It was a nightmare within a dream. I did hiss, though, which causes Georgie to stir.

"Hissy?" she asks groggily.

I wriggle against her, letting her know that, yes, it's me. I'm hoping that she's too drowsy to wake up, that she'll drop back to sleep. I purr, hoping it will lull her.

She sets her hand on my back. It's heavy with slumber. I think I'm okay.

She abruptly brings her knee upward, into my belly. I stifle a groan. I scoot out from under her hand, away from the knee, toward her chest. She lies still. She's drifting off. I close my eyes. She twists, her right arm swinging through the air, pulling her onto her other side. I edge up to her back, which is now next to me. This tossing and turning could go on for a while. Should I leap to the chair?

No, I'll stick it out.

Her breathing again deepens, and she seems as lifeless as a rag doll. I lie as still as I can, waiting. After a minute or two, I allow myself to believe the scuffle is over.

I close my eyes and hope for more restful dreams.

I am in a rocking rowboat, but I am not seasick. I sit at the back of the boat, on a wooden bench. I hold my head high and breathe in the salty sea air. It's refreshing. I widen my eyes and gaze out at the horizon. If I can keep from falling asleep in my dream, I may just get the sleep I need.

25.

Up

"Hissy cat!" Zeb yells.

I open my eyes.

Zeb is up.

So is the sun, and Georgie.

So am I.

It's another day, wide awake, with the Fitzes.

Hsssssssssss!

ACKNOWLEDGMENTS

Thanks to the writers of
West Hills Middle School, 2012.